Journey to Jo'burg

A SOUTH AFRICAN STORY

with Related Readings

Glencoe
McGraw-Hill

New York, New York Columbus, Ohio Woodland Hills, California Peoria, Illinois

Acknowledgments

Grateful acknowledgment is given authors, publishers, photographers, museums, and agents for permission to reprint the following copyrighted material. Every effort has been made to determine copyright owners. In case of any omissions, the Publisher will be pleased to make suitable acknowledgments in future editions.

Journey to Jo'burg by Beverly Naidoo. Copyright © 1986 by Beverly Naidoo. Used by permission of HarperCollins Publishers.

"The Road to Freedom" by Myles Gordon, from *Scholastic Update*, Feburary 25, 1994. Copyright © 1994 by Scholastic, Inc. Reprinted by permission.

"Children of Apartheid" by Ettagale Blauer, from *Scholastic Update*, February 25, 1994. Copyright © 1994 by Scholastic, Inc. Reprinted by permission.

"They Have Not Been Able/No Han Podido" from *Landscape and Exile* by Armando Valladares and edited by Marguerite Bouvard. Copyright © 1985. Reprinted by permission of Rowan Tree Press.

Cover Art: *Fan Seller*, 1995, Andrew Macara. Oil on canvas 63.5 x 76.2 cm. Private Collection/Bridgeman Art Library

NOTE: *In this novel, the writer shows the effects of apartheid on a family in South Africa. Some words, references, and situations may offend certain readers.*

Glencoe/McGraw-Hill

A Division of The McGraw·Hill Companies

Send all inquiries to:
Glencoe/McGraw-Hill
8787 Orion Place
Columbus, OH 43240

ISBN 0-07-826219-4
Printed in the United States of America
6 7 8 9 026 10 09 08

Contents

Journey to Jo'burg: A South African Story

Chapter 1	Naledi's Plan	1
Chapter 2	The Road	3
Chapter 3	Oranges!	5
Chapter 4	Ride on a Truck	8
Chapter 5	The City of Gold	11
Chapter 6	A New Friend	13
Chapter 7	Mma	16
Chapter 8	The Police	19
Chapter 9	The Photograph	22
Chapter 10	Grace's Story	24
Chapter 11	Journey Home	26
Chapter 12	The Hospital	29
Chapter 13	Life and Death	32
Chapter 14	Waiting	34
Chapter 15	Hope	36

Continued

Contents *Continued*

Related Readings

Myles Gordon	**The Road to Freedom**	magazine article	**41**
Ettagale Blauer	**Children of Apartheid**	magazine article	**47**
Judy Boppell Peace	*from* **The Boy Child Is Dying**	anecdote	**51**
Ranjit Warrier	**Jargon from ISL (ISLESE)**	Web site	**59**
Armando Valladares	**They Have Not Been Able/ No Han Podido**	poem	**64**

Journey to Jo'burg

A SOUTH AFRICAN STORY

Beverley Naidoo

*In memory of two small children who died far
away from their mother . . . and to Mary,
their Mma, who worked in Jo'burg.*

Chapter 1 | Naledi's Plan

NALEDI AND TIRO were worried. Their baby sister, Dineo, was ill, very ill. For three days now, Nono, their granny, had been trying to cool her fever with damp cloths placed on her little head and body. Mmangwane, their aunt, made her take sips of water, but still their sister lay hot and restless, crying softly at times.

"Can't we take Dineo to the hospital?" Naledi begged, but Nono said Dineo was much too sick to be carried that far. The only hospital was many kilometers away, and Naledi also knew they had no money to pay a doctor to visit them. No one in the village had that much money.

"If only Mma was here," Naledi wished over and over as she and Tiro walked down to the village tap with their empty buckets. She tightly clutched the coins in her hand.

Each morning the children had to pass the place of graves on their way to buy the day's water, and only last week another baby in the village had died. It was always scary seeing the little graves, but especially this fresh one now.

As they came nearer, Naledi fixed her eyes on the ground ahead, trying not to look, trying not to think. But it was no use. She just couldn't stop herself thinking of her own little sister being lowered into a hole in the ground.

Finally Naledi could stand it no longer. When they had returned with the water, she called Tiro to the back of the house and spoke bluntly.

"We must get Mma, or Dineo is going to die!"

"But how?" Tiro was bewildered.

Their mother worked and lived in Johannesburg, more than 300 kilometers away.

"We can get to the big road and walk," Naledi replied calmly.

It was school vacation now, but during the term it took the children more than an hour to walk to school each day, so they were used to walking. Naledi wasn't going to let herself think how much longer it would take to get to Johannesburg.

Tiro, however, was not so sure.

"But Nono doesn't want us to worry Mma and I know she won't let us go!"

"That's just it," Naledi retorted quickly. "Nono and Mmangwane keep saying Dineo will be better soon. You heard them talking last night. They say they don't want to send Mma a telegram and frighten her. But what if they wait and it's too late?"

Tiro thought for a moment.

"Can't we send Mma a telegram?"

"How can we if we haven't the money? And if we borrow some, Nono will hear about it and be very cross with us."

It was clear that Naledi had made up her mind—and Tiro knew his sister. She was four years older than him, already thirteen, and once she had decided something, that was that.

So Tiro gave up reasoning.

The children went to find Naledi's friend Poleng, and explained. Poleng was very surprised but agreed to help. She would tell Nono once the children had gone and she also promised to help their granny by bringing the water and doing the other jobs.

"How will you eat on the way?" Poleng asked.

Tiro looked worried, but Naledi was confident.

"Oh, we'll find something."

Poleng told them to wait and ran into her house, returning soon with a couple of sweet potatoes and a bottle of water. The children thanked her. She was indeed a good friend.

Before they could go, Naledi had to get the last letter Mma had sent, so they would know where to look for her in the big city. Slipping into the house, Naledi took the letter quietly from the tin without Nono or Mmangwane noticing. Both were busy with Dineo as Naledi slipped out again.

Chapter 2 | The Road

THE CHILDREN WALKED QUICKLY away from the village. The road was really just a track made by car tires—two lines of dusty red earth leading out across the flat, dry grassland.

Once at the big tar road, they turned in the direction of the early morning sun, for that was the way to Johannesburg. The steel railway line glinted alongside the road.

"If only we had some money to buy tickets for the train. We don't have even one cent." Tiro sighed.

"Never mind. We'll get there somehow!" Naledi was still confident as they set off eastward.

The tar road burned their feet.

"Let's walk at the side," Tiro suggested.

The grass was dry and scratchy, but they were used to it. Now and again, a car or a truck roared by, and the road was quiet again and they were alone. Naledi began to sing the words of her favorite tune and Tiro was soon joining in.

On they walked.

"Can't we stop and eat?" Tiro was beginning to feel sharp stabs of hunger. But Naledi wanted to go on until they reached the top of the long, low hill ahead.

Their legs slowed down as they began the walk uphill, their bodies feeling heavy. At last they came to the top and flopped down to rest.

Hungrily they ate their sweet potatoes and drank the water. The air was hot and still. Some birds skimmed lightly across the sky as they gazed down at the long road ahead. It stretched into the distance, between fenced-off fields and dry grass, up to another far-off hill.

"Come on! We must get on," Naledi insisted, pulling herself up quickly.

She could tell that Tiro was already tired, but they couldn't afford to stop for long. The sun had already passed its midday position, and they didn't seem to have traveled very far.

On they walked, steadily, singing to break the silence.

But in the middle of the afternoon, when the road led into a small town, they stopped singing and began to walk a little faster. They were afraid a policeman might stop them because they were strangers.

Policemen were dangerous. Even in their village they knew that. . . .

The older children at school had made up a song:

> Beware that policeman,
> He'll want to see your pass,
> He'll say it's not in order,
> That day may be your last!

Grown-ups were always talking about this "pass." If you wanted to visit some place, the pass must allow it. If you wanted to change your job, the pass must allow it. It seemed everyone in school knew somebody who had been in trouble over the pass.

Naledi and Tiro remembered all too clearly the terrible stories their uncle had told them about a prison farm. One day he had left his pass at home and a policeman had stopped him. That was how he got sent to the prison farm.

So, without even speaking, Naledi and Tiro knew the fear in the other's heart as they walked through the strange town. They longed to look in some of the shop windows, but they did not dare stop. Nervously they hurried along the main street, until they had left the last house of the town behind them.

Chapter 3 | Oranges!

ON THEY WALKED. The sun was low down now, and there was a strong smell of oranges coming from rows and rows of orange trees behind barbed-wire fences. As far as they could see there were orange trees with dark green leaves and bright round fruit. Oranges were sweet and wonderful to taste and they didn't have them often.

The children looked at each other.

"Do you think we could . . ." Tiro began.

But Naledi was already carefully pushing apart the barbed wire, edging her body through.

"Keep watch!" she ordered Tiro.

She was on tiptoe, stretching for an orange, when they heard, "HEY YOU!"

Naledi dropped down, then dashed for the fence. Tiro was holding the wires for her. She tried to scramble through, but it was too late. A hand grasped her and pulled her back.

Naledi looked up and saw a young boy, her own age.

"What are you doing?" he demanded.

He spoke in Tswana, their own language.

"The white farmer could kill you if he sees you. Don't you know he has a gun to shoot thieves?"

"We're not thieves. We've been walking all day and we're very hungry. Please don't call him," Naledi pleaded.

The boy looked more friendly now and asked where they came from.

So they told him about Dineo and how they were going to Johannesburg. The boy whistled.

"Phew. So far!"

He paused.

"Look. I know a place where you can sleep tonight and where the farmer won't find you. Stay here and I'll take you there when it's dark."

Naledi and Tiro glanced at each other, still a little nervous.

"Don't worry. You'll be safe waiting here. The farmer has gone inside for his supper," the boy reassured them. Then he grinned. "But if you eat oranges you must hide the peels well or there will be big trouble. We have to pick the fruit, but we're not allowed to eat it."

He turned and ran off, calling softly, "See you later."

"Can we stay here for the night?" Tiro asked.

Naledi wasn't too sure if they should.

"It can go badly if the farmer finds us. Remember what happened to Poleng's brother?"

When Poleng's brother had been caught taking a *mielie*, the poor boy had been whipped until he couldn't stand up anymore.

Tiro bit his lip.

"But we can leave early in the morning before the farmer is up, can't we?"

"Well . . . I expect we must sleep somewhere, or we'll be too tired to walk tomorrow," Naledi agreed slowly.

So Tiro slipped through the barbed wire and together they picked some oranges. It seemed a bit safer now that it was getting darker. Four large oranges were enough for Naledi, but Tiro kept on picking and eating more.

"You'll be sick if you stuff yourself like that," warned his sister.

Still he took no notice, until suddenly he clutched his tummy.

"Ooooh!" he groaned.

Naledi just said, "What did I tell you? Come on, we must hide the peels."

With two sharp stones they began to dig a hole. Tiro made odd little grunts from the pain in his tummy, but he dug well even though the ground was hard and dry. After burying the peels and filling up the hole, they searched around for stones and dry leaves to cover over the freshly dug soil.

They sat close together, shivering a little from the night chill. Naledi had begun to wonder if the boy really would return, when they heard the sound of soft running footsteps. The shape in the dark was that of the boy worker.

"Come!" He beckoned, and began to lead the way through rows and rows of orange trees.

They stumbled along, hardly able to see, but at last they came to a shed.

"You'll be warm with the sacks," the boy said quietly as he let them in. Then, shyly, he took out a tin plate from under a sack. "I brought you a little pap. I'm sorry, but that's all we get here most days."

"Thank you, thank you," Tiro and Naledi whispered.

"*Sala sentle*," said the boy as he slipped away in the dark.

"*Tsamaya sentle*," came the reply from the shed.

Ride on a Truck

Chapter 4

TIRO WOKE when he heard the rooster crow. The shed was already half light. He shook Naledi.

"Get up! We must hurry!"

As they crept out from the shed, they saw the farm buildings a little distance away, with thin smoke rising from the chimney.

Silently they ran through the long grass toward the orange trees. Then through the orange trees, row after row, until there at last was the barbed wire.

Finding the road again, they almost felt happy! The road was cool from the night and they sang as they walked.

The sun rose higher. On they walked. The heat sank into them and they felt the sweat on their bodies. On they walked. Alone again, except for the odd flashing by of a car or a truck.

SCREECH! Tires skidded and stopped.

"Where are you two kids going?"

The driver of the truck stuck a friendly face out the window.

"To Johannesburg, Rra."

"Are you crazy? That's more than two hundred fifty kilometers away!"

"We have to go," Naledi said simply, and explained.

"Well, well, that's something!" the driver muttered.

"It will take you about a week to walk that far and your granny will be very worried. I should take you back home, but I'm late today already."

He paused to think.

"Do you know where your mother works?"

Naledi nodded, pulling out the letter from her pocket.

"All right then. Hop on the back and I'll take you to Jo'burg. I'm taking the oranges there."

"Thank you, Rra!"

The children laughed. They pulled themselves up onto the truck, wedging themselves against the sacks of oranges. So they were really on their way! And it was their first time on a truck too!

The engine started up and the lorry was soon thundering along. Walking had been so quiet, but traveling in a lorry was very noisy. The air, which had been so hot and still before, now swept past their faces. The land, which had stood still, now seemed to rush by.

Thornbushes, telegraph poles, wire fences, plowed fields, cattle, rows of oranges, tall gum trees by a farm house . . . Almost as soon as they had seen something, it was gone.

Little by little, Tiro began to lean farther out over the side to feel the wind on his face. Naledi called, "Sit back or you'll fall!" but her brother took no notice.

Suddenly the truck went over a bump and Tiro jerked forward. Naledi grabbed him just in time.

"Didn't I tell you?" she shouted over the noise of the lorry.

A little shaken, Tiro mumbled "Sorry" and settled back properly against the orange sacks. Together they watched the road stretching far out behind them.

As the lorry sped on its way through the countryside, the children saw how the land was changing. Where they lived the land was almost flat, with few hills. Now for the first time, they were seeing proper mountains with steep rocks and crags. In some places it looked as if the road had been cut through the rock. Naledi was wondering how people could cut through rock, when Tiro asked her, "Where shall we find Mma in Jo'burg?"

"It's a place called 'Parktown,'" she read slowly.

Tiro took the letter and studied the words too.

Naledi began to think of their mother and how, when Mma visited them, her first remarks were always about how they must work hard at school. When they had asked Mma why she worked so far away from home, her reply had been, "How else can I find the money to send you to school?"

But it was still very strange, thought Naledi.

Once she had asked Mma, "Why can't we live with you in the city? We could go to school there, couldn't we?"

Mma had seemed upset, but just said, "The white people who make the laws don't allow it. That's how it is."

But why not? Why not? thought Naledi.

Chapter 5 | The City of Gold

THE TRUCK JOLTED TO A STOP and the driver came around to the back.

"O.K.?" he asked. "You can stretch your legs for a minute."

He helped them down.

"Your truck is very fast," Tiro said.

"Yes! But it's not *my* truck. I only drive it for the *baas*."

They didn't stop for long, because the driver had to get to Johannesburg and return the same day.

"Look out for the mine dumps," he told the children, as they climbed back up. "It's the earth they dig up to get to the gold. Jo'burg is the city of gold, so they say!" He gave a dry laugh.

The children looked oddly at each other.

"What's the matter?" the driver asked.

The children were silent for a moment. Then Naledi said quietly, "Our father worked in a mine and he got sick with the coughing sickness. He died there."

"Awu! Awu! That's bad!" The driver shook his head.

The children watched out for the mine dumps. When their father was alive he used to come home once a year. He would tell them about the great dark holes and passages under the earth.

"But Rra, why do you go away for so long?" they remembered asking him.

"To get money so you can eat, my children."

Nor could they forget his last visit. The terrible coughing in the night and Nono's soft, worried voice.

Now these mountains of sand had taken their father forever. Naledi put her arms around Tiro.

* * *

The countryside disappeared, and soon buildings seemed to follow buildings without end.

"This must be Jo'burg!" exclaimed Naledi, as the truck raced along a great wide road toward tall shapes that speared up into the sky. There was noise, smoke and a horrid smell coming from the traffic. So many cars, so many people!

"How shall we find Mma?" Tiro whispered.

"We'll find her somehow," Naledi comforted him.

The truck began to slow down. The buildings now seemed to be crowding in on them. Naledi and Tiro sat tightly together, trying not to feel frightened.

Finally the truck shuddered to a complete stop and the driver came around to the back.

"This is where I unload. I would like to take you safely to your mother, but my time here is too short. Wait here while I find the right bus for you."

"But we . . ." Tiro began, but the driver had already disappeared into the crowd. He was back soon.

"There's a bus stop just around the corner for Parktown. Come, I'll show you."

"But we don't have money for the bus, so we have to walk," Tiro now managed to tell the driver.

"What children! You've got a lot of guts, but you know nothing about Jo'burg. It's dangerous! You can't walk here on your own. Here—take this!"

He pushed a few coins into Naledi's hand, and before the children had finished thanking him, he began to steer them through the crowd.

At the bus stop he explained how they must say where they were going and ask where to get off the bus.

"You don't need to wait with us here, Rra. We'll be all right now," Naledi assured the driver.

He didn't seem happy about leaving them on their own, but Naledi insisted they could manage. It would be too bad if he got into trouble. The children thanked him again and they made their farewells, before he was swallowed up once more among the city people.

Chapter 6 | A New Friend

As they turned toward the road, there was a bus with the word "PARKTOWN" in big letters on the front. It was slowing down a little way up the road and the doors were opening. Through the front windscreen they could see the driver was black.

"Come on, Tiro!" called Naledi, pulling him by the arm. They were just about to jump aboard, when someone shouted at them in English, "What's wrong with you? Are you stupid?"

Startled, they looked up at the angry face of the bus driver and then at the bus again. White faces stared at them from inside as the bus moved off.

Naledi and Tiro stood on the side of the road, shaken, holding hands tightly, when a voice behind them said, "Don't let it bother you. That's what they're like. You'd better come out of the road."

A young woman put out her hand to bring them onto the pavement.

"You must be strangers here if you don't know about the buses. This stop has a white sign, but we have to wait by the black one over there."

She pointed to a small black metal signpost.

"You must also look at the front of the bus for the small notice saying 'Non-whites only.'"

"I'm sorry. We forgot to look," Naledi explained.

"It's not you who should be sorry!" said the young woman forcefully. "They should be sorry, those stupid people! Why shouldn't we use any bus? When our buses are full, their buses are half empty. Don't you be sorry!"

The children glanced at each other. This person was different from their mother. Mma never spoke out like that.

The young woman asked where they were going. Naledi took out the letter, and when the young woman looked at the address, she exclaimed, "But this is near where my mother works. I'm on my way to visit her today, so I can show you the place."

"Thank you, Mma." The children smiled. Lucky again.

"By the way, I'm Grace Mbatha. Now who are you both, and where are you from? You speak Tswana the way my mother does. Maybe you live near my mother's people."

So, once again, the children began their story.

Luckily the bus wasn't full when it arrived. Grace had warned them that in the rush hour you were almost squeezed to death. As the bus trundled along, stopping and starting with the traffic, there was a chance to stare out the windows. Tiro thought the cyclists were very brave, riding in between all the cars. Naledi kept trying to see the tops of the tall buildings, twisting her neck around until it began to hurt!

The bus now heaved its way up a steep hill and soon they were leaving the city buildings, seeing the sky again, as well as trees, grass lawns and flowers either side of the road. Behind the trees were big houses, such as they had never seen before. Grace smiled at the way the children were staring, amazed.

"Don't you know the people in this place have a lot of money? My mother looks after two children in a very big house, and there is another person just to cook, and another person to look after the garden."

Naledi and Tiro listened with interest. Mma never liked to talk much to them about her work when she was at home, although once they had overheard Mma talking to Nono about the child whom she looked after. Mma had said, "The little girl is very rude. She thinks I belong to her mother. You should hear how she can shout at me."

Naledi wanted to ask Grace to tell them some more, but she was still a little shy, and soon they had reached their stop.

They stepped off the bus onto a wide pavement along a street lined with great leafy trees.

"That's the road where your mother works at number twenty-five. My mma works at number seventeen in the next road down there. Can you manage now?"

The children nodded, and then Grace added, "If you need somewhere to stay tonight, you can come back with me to Soweto. I'm going home at six o'clock, O.K.?"

Tiro and Naledi thanked Grace, although they were a little puzzled about needing somewhere to stay. After all, they would be with their mother now and they would be going home with her as quickly as possible, back to Dineo.

As they turned to go down the road, they suddenly felt very excited—and anxious too. So much had been happening that they hadn't been thinking all along of their little sister.

Please let her be all right now pounded in Naledi's brain.

Half walking, half running, they made for number 25.

Chapter 7 | Mma

THERE IT STOOD, a great pink house with its own grass lawn and trees in front, even its own road leading up to the front door! The two children stopped at the wide iron gates, looking up to it. The gates were closed, with a notice on them: "BEWARE OF THE DOG."

"Are we allowed in?" Tiro whispered.

"We must go in," Naledi replied, opening the gate a little.

Nervously they slipped in and slowly walked up the drive to the large front door. Before they dared to knock, they heard a fierce barking from inside, which made them grip each other's hands, ready to run back to the street. Then they heard a sharp voice inside call out, in English, "Joyce, see who it is!"

The door opened.

As Mma gasped, the children flung themselves at her and she clasped them in her arms, hugging them. Tears welled up in her eyes as the children sobbed against her.

"What is wrong? What is wrong?" Mma cried softly.

"Who is it, Joyce?" came a brisk voice from behind. The dog was still barking.

"Be quiet, Tiger!" ordered the brisk voice, and the barking stopped.

Mma stifled her sobs.

"Madam, these are my children."

"What are they doing here?" asked the white lady.

"Madam, I don't know. They haven't told me yet."

"Dineo is very ill, Mma." Naledi spoke between sobs. "Her fever won't go away. Nono and Mmangwane don't want to trouble you, but I told Tiro we must come and bring you home."

Mma gasped again and held her children more tightly.

"Madam, my little girl is very sick. Can I go home to see her?"

The Madam raised her eyebrows.

"Well, Joyce, I can't possibly let you go today. I need you tonight to stay in with Belinda. The Master and I are going to a very important dinner party."

She paused.

"But I suppose you can go tomorrow."

"Thank you, Madam."

"I hope you realize how inconvenient this will be for me. If you are not back in a week, I shall just have to look for another maid, you understand?"

"Yes, Madam."

The children couldn't follow everything the Madam was saying in English, but her voice sounded annoyed, while Mma spoke so softly. Why does the white lady seem cross with Mma? It's not Mma's fault that Dineo is sick, Naledi thought.

The children huddled close to Mma's starched white apron. They hadn't seen her in this strange servant's uniform before.

As Mma led the children through to the kitchen, they glanced across at open doors leading into other large rooms. A wide staircase also led upward. Never had they imagined a house could be this size!

In the kitchen Mma gave them a drink of water and some porridge she had cooked earlier. The kitchen seemed like a picture out of a magazine Mma had once brought home from the Madam. Their mother must have been busy cleaning that afternoon, because glistening plates of different sizes, cups and saucers, and delicate glasses were neatly stacked close to a large empty cupboard.

Naledi noticed that Mma took the tin plates and mugs for them from a separate little cupboard. While they ate, Mma quickly got on with her work.

When she had finished, she took the children to her room at the back of the yard. The children looked around the little room with interest. On the big iron bed was a white cover which Mma had neatly embroidered. It must be strange sleeping all on your own, thought Tiro. At home they all shared a room.

When the children noticed the electric light, Mma said they could try it. But after Tiro had flicked it on and off about ten times, Mma told him to stop.

Bringing the children close to her now, Mma sat down at last and asked them to tell her fully what had happened.

The Madam had made it clear to Mma that the police wouldn't like it if the children spent the night in Parktown. So when Naledi spoke about Grace and her offer to take them to Soweto, Mma seemed of two minds. She knew Grace's mother well, but Soweto was also dangerous.

After getting the Madam's permission to go out for a little, Mma took her children by the hand and they walked to number 17 in the next road. They went around to the back of the house and found Grace still there.

"These two will be just fine with me," Grace assured Mma.

It was arranged that Grace and the children would meet Mma at Johannesburg station at seven the next morning. Mma gave Grace some money for the fares and, close to tears again, she hugged the children good-bye.

"Cheer up, you two," said Grace. "You can come and meet my brothers."

Chapter 8 | The Police

IT WAS RUSH HOUR when they got on the train to Soweto, and the children clung tightly to Grace. There was no sitting space, and it felt as if all their breath was being squeezed out of them. Grown-up bodies pressed in from above and all around them. Some people laughed, some people swore and others kept silent, as the train shook and lurched on its way.

At each station the crowd heaved toward the carriage door, people urgently pushing their way through. Naledi and Tiro tried to press backward to stay close to Grace.

But in a sudden surge at one of the stations, they found themselves being carried forward, hurling out onto the platform. Desperately they tried to reach back to the open door, but passengers were still coming out, although the train was already beginning to move on.

Naledi was just able to see Grace wedged inside. She was trying to get out, but the train was on its way! Naledi and Tiro looked at each other in dismay. What now?

Everyone was walking toward the stairs which led to a bridge over the railway line. Soon the platform would be empty and the guard would see them. No tickets, no money, no idea of how they could find Grace. They would have to wait until she came back to get them, yet there was nowhere to hide on the platform.

"Let's go and look from the bridge," Naledi suggested.

Suddenly, without any warning, there was a commotion up ahead. Three figures in uniform stood at the top of the stairs.

Police!

People began turning around and coming rapidly back down. Some began running along the platform toward a high barbed-wire fence at the other end. The runners leapt at the fence and scrambled over it.

Others jumped down to the track, sprinted over the railway lines and clambered up to the opposite platform. But just as they got there, more policemen appeared on that side.

"Where can we go?" Tiro urgently tugged at his sister's hand.

"We'll have to slip past them," she whispered, pulling him toward the stairs.

Some people were feeling into pockets, others frantically searching through bags.

Pass raid!

A man was protesting loudly that he had left his pass at home. It would only take two minutes to get it. The police could come and see, or someone could call his child to bring it. He cried out his address, once, twice . . . Slap!

"*Hou jou bek*," barked the white officer in charge. His blue eyes stared coldly as a black policeman pushed the man against the wall.

One at a time people were pulled forward to be checked. When a boy said that he wasn't yet sixteen, the policeman just yelled he was a "liar" and a "loafer." Tiro felt his heart freeze, but the boy didn't cry. Instead his eyes seemed to have fire in them as he was handcuffed.

A voice in the crowd shouted, "Shame! Locking up children!"

As the muttering grew louder, a woman spotted Naledi and Tiro and screamed, "You'll say these kids are sixteen next!"

The white officer took a threatening step forward. He looked murderous. Then, glancing at the children, he made a sign with his hand for them to go through.

"We can't stay on the bridge while the police are here," panted Naledi when they had got past. From the bridge they could see the road outside the railway station. Next to a large van were more police. An old woman was being pushed inside the van. Tiro looked back at the people in handcuffs on the bridge.

"Why don't we run and call the child to bring his father's pass? We heard the address, so we can find it."

"Let's hurry then!" agreed Naledi.

Once past the police van, they asked a lady selling apples at the roadside to point out the way. The children weaved in and out among people as they ran along the stony road, between rows of gray block houses all looking exactly alike. No great leafy trees here, only gray smoke settling everywhere.

When they reached the right number house, they found a boy struggling with a heavy tub. As soon as he understood their message, he dashed into the house, and a minute later came rushing out with a book in his hand.

All three raced back down the road, but just as they came in sight of the station, there was the big police van pulling off.

The boy shouted at it as it sped past them, carrying away his father. He flung the pass down, picked up a stone and let it fly at the van. The van swung around the corner, the stone just grazing the mudguard.

"I'll burn this one day!" stormed the boy, picking up his father's pass. "How can our parents put up with it?" There was fury in his voice. Then it became gentler. "Thanks anyway for trying. . . . I must go and tell my mother now."

The children stood silently watching as he walked back home.

"Naledi! Tiro!"

Startled, they looked around to find from where the voice was coming. It sounded quite far off.

Looking up toward the railway bridge, they saw Grace waving. Quickly they ran back to the station.

Grace came down with their tickets to get them through. It was a relief to be with her again.

"This time I'm really going to hold on to you," she told them, taking each firmly by the hand.

"Do you know what happened to us, Mma?" Tiro was anxious to tell Grace all.

Chapter 9

The Photograph

WHEN AT LAST they arrived at Grace's house, two boys, a little younger than Tiro, came racing out, then stopped short to look at Naledi and Tiro.

"Paul, Jonas. I've brought some friends for you," Grace announced.

Her brothers smiled shyly.

Inside, the house was dark until Grace lit a lamp. The small room was almost filled by a table, a cupboard and stove.

"Hungry?" asked Grace. Four heads nodded.

It wasn't long before a good smell of beans was coming from the pot. Jonas and Paul brought out some wire cars and the younger children were soon busy discussing different things they had made, while Grace chatted with Naledi.

Before the meal, hands had to be washed at the tap outside the back door.

"Our people wash and clean up for others all day, but look how we must wash ourselves!" Grace spoke sharply.

Naledi wanted to ask Grace what she meant, but Tiro had begun splashing water.

"Stop it, Tiro! You're wasting water." Naledi made him come away from the tap. She explained how they had to buy water from the village tap at home.

"We used to get our water from the river, but it's all dried up now."

"Was your river very big?"

"Were there crocodiles?" Paul and Jonas, who had never been beyond Johannesburg, were curious!

It was while they were eating that Naledi noticed a small photograph on the wall of Grace's mother with four children. It had been taken some years ago, when Paul and Jonas were no more than babies.

"Who's this?" Naledi enquired, pointing to a boy who looked a few years older than Grace.

"That's our eldest brother, Dumi, but he isn't here anymore," replied Grace rather quietly.

"Where is he?" asked Tiro.

"If I tell you, you mustn't go shouting about it."

Naledi and Tiro shook their heads.

"But remember what Mma said, Grace. We mustn't talk about it, or Dumi will be in trouble." Paul looked very worried.

"It's all right," his older sister assured him. "These two aren't big mouths like some kids round here."

By now Tiro and Naledi were looking quite puzzled.

"You see," Grace began, "our brother Dumi got picked up by the police, in '76. That was the time when the students here and all over were marching, and the place was on fire. . . ."

Grace paused.

"You must know about it. Or were you too young then?"

"The older students at school sometimes talk about such things, but we don't know much," Naledi admitted.

So, with the dim light from the lamp flickering their shadows on the walls of the small room, Grace began to tell the children her story.

Chapter 10 | Grace's Story

IT WAS A "TIME OF FIRE," as Grace called it, when she and Dumi had marched in the streets with thousands of other schoolchildren. They were protesting that their schools taught them only what the white government wanted them to know.

On the banner that Dumi and his friends carried, they had written:

BLACKS ARE NOT DUSTBINS.

Everything went all right until the police saw the schoolchildren marching, and then the trouble started. The police aimed their guns and began to shoot with real bullets, killing whoever was in the way.

It was terrible. The police shot tear gas too, making everyone's eyes burn.

People were screaming, bleeding, falling. More police came in great steel tanks, and more in helicopters, firing from above. A little girl, about eight years old, standing near Grace raised her fist, and next thing she was lying dead.

People became fighting mad, throwing stones at the police, burning down schools and government offices. Smoke and flames were everywhere.

But the police kept shooting, until hundreds were dead. Hundreds were hurt and hundreds were arrested.

Dumi was one of those arrested.

When he came out of prison, he said that the police had beaten him up badly, but he would go on fighting even if they killed him.

Then one night he disappeared. When their mother went to each police station, asking if he was there, the police said "No." But maybe they were lying. Maybe they had killed him too.

For a year they had no news.

Until one day a letter came. It was from Dumi. There was no address, but it had been mailed in Johannesburg. Dumi wrote that he was well and studying in another country. He was giving the letter to a friend to mail. He also wrote that he would be coming back one day. Coming back to help fight for freedom and make life better for everyone. He had written FREEDOM in big letters.

The family had been so excited that he was alive, so worried about the dangers he faced, yet so proud of his courage. Dumi had been a boy when he left, but now he would be a man. Although it was a long time since they had heard from him, they hadn't given up hope. They were still waiting.

When Grace finished talking, the children remained quite silent.

"Well, it's time to sleep," Grace said, pushing back her chair and stretching herself up. Her young brothers cleared up the dishes, stacking them up ready to wash them outside in the morning.

Grace shared her bed with Naledi and the boys shared theirs with Tiro. He was soon fast asleep, but Naledi lay awake for a while, thinking.

So much had happened. She wondered what her mother was doing. Was Mma alone in the little room in the yard, or was she still watching over the child in the big house?

Naledi was sure Mma must be thinking of Dineo. Why couldn't Mma have left straight away, and what if something happened to Dineo before they arrived? Naledi didn't want to think about that. At least the delay had led to them being with Grace, and she really liked Grace.

Her mind wandered over the terrible events in Soweto, to Dumi and to the word in big letters—freedom. What did the word really mean? Did it mean they could live with their mother? Did it mean they could go to secondary school? But Grace said the children marched because they had to learn a lot of "rubbish" in school. So what would you learn in a school with freedom?

There were so many questions, Naledi thought, as she drifted into sleep.

Journey Home

Chapter 11

WAKE UP! It's five o'clock."

When Grace's voice reached Naledi and Tiro, they pulled themselves up. Silently they drank the tea Grace had made, before slipping quietly out of the house, leaving Jonas and Paul still asleep.

It was half dark, but already many people were hurrying toward the station, and the train was crowded all over again. Most of the faces still looked tired. Bones squeezed against bones as they jolted, jerked and swayed with each movement of the train. At each station yet more bodies crammed in against them, until at last they were thrown out with the crowd rushing off to another day's work in Johannesburg.

When they arrived at the main ticket office, Mma was already waiting with her case. She thanked Grace warmly.

"Anytime you need help, let me know," Mma added.

"*Tsamaya sentle,*" Grace called as they parted at the barrier.

"*Sala sentle!*" They waved good-bye as they went.

The train going home wasn't crowded so the children sat by the window, hoping to see places they had passed on the way, especially the orange farm where they had spent the night. They told Mma about the boy who had helped them. She said quietly, "That was brave of him. He could have got into a lot of trouble."

"Mma, do you know Grace has a br . . ."

Tiro was beginning to talk about Dumi, but Naledi quickly nudged him with her foot and gave him a stern look. The scatterbrain! Already he was forgetting the promise they had made Grace. Tiro bit his lip, but fortunately Mma hadn't noticed anything.

"Those children should be in school," Mma continued, still thinking about the boy on the farm.

Naledi lay with her head against her mother's shoulder. It was so confusing. Here was Mma saying that children should be in school, and there was Grace saying that schools taught black children rubbish.

26   JOURNEY TO JO'BURG

Didn't Dumi and his friends carry a poster saying "BLACKS ARE NOT DUSTBINS"?

What did Mma think about that and all the shooting? Had she heard about the little girl who was killed close to Grace? Mma had never spoken to them about such things. Did she think they were too young to be told?

Naledi stared out the window, without seeing anything. Her mind was too full of questions. Surely she could talk to Mma about what was troubling her? As she leant against Mma's body and felt its warmth, it seemed silly to hold back problems. Especially when their time together was so short.

"Mma . . ." Naledi began, turning to look up at her mother's face. "Grace told us how the schoolchildren marched in the streets . . ."

Naledi stopped, seeing shock and pain flash through Mma's eyes. She became even more alarmed when Mma remained quite silent for what seemed like an age, gazing down at her lap.

At last, Mma spoke very softly. "Do you know how many children died on those streets? Do you know how many mothers were crying, 'Where's my child?'"

Mma was shaking her head slowly. There was another long pause, as if she was thinking whether to say any more. Then she leant forward and covered her face with one hand, wiping her forehead.

"You know, every day I must struggle . . . struggle . . . to make everything just how the Madam wants it. The cooking, the cleaning, the washing, the ironing. From seven every morning, sometimes till ten, even eleven at night, when they have parties. The only time I sit is when I eat! But I keep quiet and do everything, because if I lose my job I won't get another one. This Madam will say I am no good. Then there will be no food for you, no clothes for you, no school for you."

Mma pulled her back up straight and put an arm around the children. Tiro shifted to come closer.

"It's very bad, Mma," Naledi said, in a low voice.

"Yes, it's bad. But those children who marched in the streets don't want to be like us . . . learning in school just how to be servants. They want to change what is wrong . . . even if they must die!"

"Oh Mma, oh Mma," Naledi whispered.

Tiro clutched Mma's hand and she pulled him toward her lap.

"What did their parents say?" he asked.

"Some tried to stop their children so they wouldn't get hurt, but there were also parents who helped them."

Mma explained how the children had asked their parents not to work on certain days, and how many people had stayed at home. It had been a time of terrible worry for Mma's friends who had families in Soweto. The eldest Mbatha boy had been arrested, and Mma told them about his mother's dreadful search at all the police stations.

So . . . Mma knew something about Dumi, Naledi thought. But neither she nor Tiro broke their own promise.

When Mma finished speaking, they sat in silence. They watched the train stop at stations on the way, passengers climbing in and out with cases, bags, and bundles.

Vast stretches of land flashed by; grassland, mountains, grassland again. Naledi suddenly felt very small. Before this journey to fetch Mma, she had never imagined that all this land existed. Nor had she any idea of what the city was like. She had never known a person like Grace before, and she had never known her own mother in the way she was beginning to know her now. . . .

"That's it. I'm sure that's it!"

Tiro's voice startled Naledi from her thoughts, but already the orange farm to which he was pointing was in the distance. Mma nodded with a slight smile.

Chapter 12 | The Hospital

NONE OF THEM SPOKE after that; their thoughts all turned to Dineo. When the train pulled in at their station, Mma hurried the children out onto the platform. Outside, she spoke anxiously to a man standing against a car. After she had taken some banknotes from her purse, he agreed to take them first to their village and then on to the hospital. So much money, thought Naledi. Mma must have borrowed it.

As the car bumped along the road into the village, churning up the dust, it seemed longer than two days ago that they had set off walking. Mma directed the driver to the house and people looked up as the car passed by. It wasn't often a car came this way. The sound of the motor brought Nono and Mmangwane outside. Nono looked so thin and weary, but her eyes lit up when she saw who it was.

"The child is very sick," she whispered in a low voice.

Mma rushed in and came out clasping Dineo close to her, the little girl lying limply in Mma's arms, her eyes sunken.

"You children must stay with Nono," Mma said firmly, as they struggled to bring the case out of the car.

"Oh please, Mma, can't I come with you? Please?" Naledi pleaded. "Tiro can help Nono."

Mma looked across at Nono, whose tired face nodded yes. Naledi gave her grandmother a quick hug.

"Thank you, Nono! Tiro will tell you everything . . . and please don't be angry with us. We're very sorry we gave you more worry."

"But we had to get Mma!" put in Tiro.

"Well, come in and tell us about it," invited Mmangwane.

Nono put an arm around Tiro's shoulders as they waved good-bye. From inside the car Naledi watched the little group grow smaller until they had quite disappeared behind the clouds of dust.

As the car now jerked its way back to the town over the rough roads, Mma cradled Dineo in her arms, whispering soft words to her. Naledi held Dineo's little hand, stroking and playing gently with her fingers. But the little girl made no response. Each minute on the way to the hospital now seemed so important. What if they got there just a minute too late? That couldn't happen . . . could it?

At last they were traveling through the town, and then out into the open again, until at last there was a cluster of low white buildings with a few trees and bushes scattered among them. Some people were waiting by the roadside outside the hospital, and as soon as Mma and Naledi climbed out of the car, an old man came hobbling over to the driver. He was followed by others and almost immediately the car, packed tight with people, was rumbling off back to the town.

Naledi stayed close to Mma as she made her way past people sitting or lying down on the ground in front of the buildings. A lady with a thin blanket wrapped over her shoulders pointed the way.

Around the corner they found the queue of patients. It led up to a verandah, where a woman in white sat at a desk.

"Is that the doctor for Dineo?" Naledi whispered.

Mma shook her head. "No. We must get a card first. The doctor is inside."

The queue moved very slowly as people shuffled forward after every few minutes. Some patients, who were too weak to stand, lay wedged against the wall and had to be helped along. Just in front of Mma and Naledi was a young woman with a small baby tied in a blanket to her back. Naledi wondered if the woman or the baby was the patient.

The sun shone down on the queue. Mma tried to screen Dineo from the glare, but the heat seemed to soak in everywhere and Dineo began to whimper. Mma tried rocking her gently, while Naledi tried singing her little songs which had always made her laugh. However, now Dineo didn't even seem to hear them. . . .

When finally it was Mma's turn at the desk, Naledi relaxed a little. Now Dineo could go inside and be given medicine. But when Mma led the way down a corridor and into a room filled with far more people than had been outside, Naledi felt panic grip her.

"Are all these people before Dineo, Mma?" she cried, softly.

"They are also very sick, Naledi. We must be patient."

They were lucky to find space on a bench next to the young woman with the baby. She didn't look much older than Grace, thought Naledi.

It was the young woman who spoke first.

"It's always long to wait. I was here before with my baby and now he's sick again."

"What's the problem?" Mma asked.

"Last time the doctor said he must have more milk, but I've no money to buy it."

Mma sighed. "I think it's the same sickness with my child."

Chapter 13 | Life and Death

ALL THROUGH THE AFTERNOON, they watched the patients being called one at a time by the nurse. Once the doctor himself came out. His face seemed nearly as white as his coat, except for the dark shadows under his eyes.

By midafternoon, Dineo needed water, but when Mma carried her to a small fountain in one corner, she almost turned away. It was so dirty! Naledi came over and struggled to cup some water in her hand without touching the sides. Then she let the water dribble over Dineo's dry little lips.

Naledi now began to feel her own empty stomach twist and turn. Her last meal had been with Grace the night before. Mma seemed to read her thoughts and sent her out to see what she could buy for a few cents. When Naledi came back with three small buns, Mma offered one to the young woman. From the way she ate it, Naledi could tell that she was very hungry too.

It was only after the light had begun to fade outside that the young woman was called to take her baby to the doctor. The child had been very quiet all afternoon, wrapped snugly against its mother's back.

In a very little time the young woman came out of the doctor's room, clutching a plastic bag. Her whole body was shaking and a man close to the door caught her just as her legs gave way.

"My baby, my baby . . . he's dead, he's dead!"

Her sobs filled the waiting room. Before Mma could go to comfort her, the nurse reappeared calling for Dineo. The sobbing pierced Naledi's mind. She heard Mma telling her to stay where she was and she watched numbly as her little sister was now carried away. Then Naledi's gaze shifted to the plastic bag. The little baby had seemed to be sleeping so peacefully just a few minutes ago. Was it already dead then?

With head bowed, almost buried in the parcel, the young woman forced herself up and stumbled out of the waiting room. Naledi's eyes now fixed on the doctor's door, but instead she saw a plastic parcel being laid in a grave. It made her want to run to Mma. She sat gripping tightly onto her seat.

When Mma finally returned, her arms were empty.

"What happened, Mma?" Naledi cried.

"We must leave Dineo here and I must come back in three days . . . Her throat is very bad . . . and her body is too weak. . . ." Mma's voice sounded choked.

Before leaving, Mma had to pay at the desk. There would be more to pay later, so she checked the remaining banknotes in her purse.

"We've nothing for bus fare—we'll just have to walk home." Mma looked drained.

"But it's not so far as Jo'burg, Mma!" Naledi put her arm through Mma's. She was surprised at her own sudden confidence when only a little while ago she had wanted to run to Mma for comfort herself. Well, at least they had each other.

Outside it was dark, but the moon fortunately lit the road and Mma knew a way which avoided the town. So with arms linked, they set off on the long walk home.

On the way Naledi asked about the doctor. Mma said they were lucky because he had been very gentle with Dineo, although he looked sick himself from tiredness.

"Did he say Dineo will get better, Mma?"

"We can only hope, my child. . . ." Mma paused and pressed Naledi's hand.

"I'm thankful you came for me. We must hope the medicine will save her."

The doctor had also told Mma that Dineo needed milk, fruit and vegetables to keep her body strong.

"But he didn't tell me how to find the money to buy them all," Mma added quietly.

By the time they reached their village, the moon had moved far across the dark sky. Nono stirred as they entered the house. She had been waiting anxiously for their return. Naledi could hardly keep her eyes open while she drank the tea Nono gave her. She crept under the blanket, finishing her last mouthful.

Chapter 14 | Waiting

IT WAS USUALLY A GOOD TIME for the children when Mma was at home. First there would be the excitement of waiting for her to arrive and then the flurry of greetings, hugs and news. Later Mma would open her case and bring out the presents she had been saving for the family. On her day off in the city, she sometimes went to jumble sales to buy the clothes white people no longer wanted. Then would follow the pleasure of days when Mma would be around the house—helping Nono with the work, or playing with Dineo, and always ready to listen to the children's stories about what they had been doing.

But this time was different—like the time when Mma came just after Rra died.

The three days of waiting before Mma had to return to the hospital passed slowly. The grown-ups didn't speak of their worst fear, although Naledi saw the heavy, worried look in their eyes. Each morning Tiro asked Mma how much longer it was until she had to collect Dineo. Then, after he had helped bring the water, he would go off to play for short periods, but Naledi preferred to stay all the while at home with Mma.

On the fourth day Mma set off very early, alone. She had borrowed just enough money from a neighbor to pay for her bus fare to and from the hospital. That day seemed to pass even more slowly. Tiro stayed right outside the house fiddling with a piece of wire, changing its shape many times, then using it to draw in the sand. When Naledi wasn't busy, she came and sat on the doorstep, gazing out at the road. She forced her mind to stay blank, just searching the distance for any figures coming from the direction of the big road, where the bus would stop. She didn't want to think about what was happening in the hospital, because it would bring back the picture of the plastic bag.

From time to time, Naledi would see the vague shape of a woman appear with a baby wrapped to her back, but as she came closer, Naledi would see it wasn't Mma. It was late in the afternoon when at last there was a figure which really did seem to be Mma. Naledi called out to Nono, who was in the house, and she and Tiro began racing up the dusty road.

"It's Mma! It is!" Tiro shouted as they ran.

"Dineo's on her back!" Naledi panted.

As the two children came sprinting toward her, Mma stopped and turned a little so they could see their sister. As the children greeted her, she gave a shy smile, resting her head on Mma's shoulder.

"She's still quite weak, but her fever has gone," said Mma.

With Naledi and Tiro either side of her, Mma walked on to the house. Mmangwane came up the road, calling out in delight. Nono remained at the door, holding on to the side for support.

"My child," she whispered, as she put out her hand to touch Dineo's head.

Chapter 15 | Hope

THAT NIGHT the children found it hard to get to sleep. Mma had to return to the city the next morning, as each day she was losing pay.

There was all the borrowed money to pay back now, as well as the money to send Nono each month for food, school and all the other expenses. Mma was clearly worried about Dineo not getting enough milk. The nurse had repeated what the doctor had told Mma about Dineo needing milk, fruit and vegetables.

"But we work very hard and earn very little," Mma had said with a sigh as she cuddled Dineo, before putting her down to sleep.

Tiro had said good night but lay thinking about the boy on the orange farm. He wondered if he himself was old enough to go and find work. But he knew Mma wouldn't agree. Hadn't she said the children working on the farm should be in school?

Then he thought of Dumi and the bit in the letter about studying in another country. Studying what? Tiro wondered. He would ask Naledi tomorrow. . . .

Tomorrow he would also remake his wire car and try out Jonas and Paul's design. Putting out his arm, he touched Dineo. It was lovely knowing she was there again. If only Mma didn't have to go away now. . . .

Naledi lay awake too, listening to the murmuring voices of Nono, Mmangwane and Mma. It was so comforting to hear them all together. But tomorrow night Mma's voice would be missing.

Naledi buried her head in her arms, forcing back her tears. Crying wouldn't help. She couldn't imagine Grace crying, and Grace had to look after her young brothers and the house all by herself most of the time. Yet Grace had said things in a way that made you feel better, like when she had said, "We're pushed all over the place, but it won't be like that forever."

But when would they see Grace again? It occurred to Naledi that at least they could write to each other. Tomorrow she must ask Mma to find out Grace's address.

Then a new idea came to her. Wasn't it possible that in her own school there were people like Grace? Naledi had overheard bits of conversations among the older students, although she had never taken much notice before. But why shouldn't she begin to talk to them and become friends, even if she was a little younger? If they heard she had been to Johannesburg, they would be interested, she was sure.

What was it Mma had said about the children in Soweto? That they didn't want to learn just to be servants. Oh yes, they were right.

All of a sudden, lying there in the dark, it became so clear to Naledi. It wasn't just *their* schools they were talking about. It was *her* school too. All those lessons on writing letters . . . for jobs as servants . . . always writing how good they were at cooking, cleaning, washing, gardening . . . always ending with "Yours obediently."

Naledi had never thought about it before tonight, but never, never, had she written about wanting to be . . . say, a doctor. Yes, that's what she'd like to be. Imagine how useful it would be if she became a doctor, especially in their own village. She could even look after her own family.

For a few moments, Naledi lay imagining herself in a long white coat, in a bright room with shining cupboards all around her (like the cupboards where Mma worked). Then something jarred. . . .

She saw in her mind someone bringing her a little baby. The mother looked like the young woman in the queue at the hospital, and the baby was so thin that its little rib bones pushed up from under its skin. The mother was clearly poor and had no food for her child.

Where would she, the doctor, get food for the baby? When she opened her shining cupboards they were empty.

Naledi then began to imagine a whole line of mothers and grandmothers bringing weak, thin little babies up to her. What could she do?

For a while she felt the tears pressing on her eyelids again. No! She wouldn't give in to tears. It was just that she couldn't work this all out by herself. Well, school would be starting again in a week. That wasn't long. At break time she would go where the older students usually sat chatting. Just wait till they heard where she and Tiro had been.

Naledi turned over and stroked Dineo's cheek, making her sister smile a little in her sleep. How strange, thought Naledi. If Dineo hadn't been so terribly ill, she and Tiro would never have made the journey to get Mma. It had saved Dineo, she was sure. But also through this journey, she had begun to find out so much. . . .

The grown-up voices had stopped and Naledi heard Mma blow out the lamp and quietly shift into bed. Naledi's eyelids were heavy and she felt sleep pulling at her. She fell asleep at last, picturing her first day back at school, surrounded by friends, old and new.

Related Readings

Myles Gordon	**The Road to Freedom**	magazine article	**41**
Ettagale Blauer	**Children of Apartheid**	magazine article	**47**
Judy Boppell Peace	*from* **The Boy Child Is Dying**	anecdote	**51**
Ranjit Warrier	**Jargon from ISL (ISLESE)**	Web site	**59**
Armando Valladares	**They Have Not Been Able/ No Han Podido**	poem	**64**

Myles Gordon

The Road to Freedom

Apartheid flourished as the result of hundreds of years of racism and oppression. However, just a few years after the events described in Journey to Jo'burg, *the apartheid system crumbled. This article was published in 1994.*

O N APRIL 27, South Africans of all races will go to the polls in the first free and democratic elections in the nation's history. The event marks the literal passing into history of the old South Africa and the birth of the new. But the new South Africa inherits a legacy of violence, ethnic hatred, oppression—and heroism—that dates back more than three centuries to the arrival of the first European settlers. The new black-led government must deal especially with the legacy of apartheid, a uniquely evil system in which all South Africans, and all aspects of South African life, were categorized by race—from where people could work, live, or go to school, to whom they could marry.

It is this system that is coming to an end with South Africa's elections. But how did such a system ever develop? Why did it last so long and what caused it to finally crumble? In the following timeline we'll retrace the incredible story of South Africa's march to freedom.

1652-1846
The Europeans Arrive

"Although descended from God, the Khoikhoi show so little of humanity that, truly, they more resemble unreasonable beasts than reasonable man." *—Wouter Schouten, Dutch settler, after meeting indigenous South Africans (1665)*

"My masters, though we fight back with all our skill, you see that the world is tumbling about our ears."—Sebetwane, leader of the Makolo people, speaking to fellow chiefs after being attacked by Dutch settlers (1837)

During the 1600s, Europeans were venturing across the globe in tall masted ships in search of exotic goods and lands to colonize. Around the same time that European settlers arrived in North America, they landed at the Cape of Good Hope, at the southern tip of Africa.

In 1652, the Dutch set up a colony and supply station there for their ships. They were followed by the French and Germans. The Europeans drove the native Khoikhoi people off the land they had lived on for more than a thousand years. Soon the native culture and economy collapsed. The whites—who shunned manual labor—brought in slaves from southeast Asia, India, and other parts of Africa to do the work.

By the early 1700s, slaves outnumbered the colony's whites, and intermarriage was common. The children of such marriages—considered neither white nor black—became known as "coloreds."

Some Dutch settlers struck out on their own and left the coastal trading post for the interior, inhabited by black tribes—the ancestors of today's black South Africans. There, the Dutch tended cattle and farmed, living in isolation in a way not unlike the Africans who surrounded them. They developed their own culture and beliefs, including a strict form of Protestantism that portrayed them as a chosen people in a hostile world. They called themselves Afrikaners—Africa's "white tribe." The language they developed was a mixture of Dutch and African languages they called "Afrikaans."

In 1795, Britain, then the world's strongest power, seized the Cape colony, establishing their own laws, and banning slavery. They looked down on the rude, mostly illiterate, Afrikaner Boers, or farmers. To escape English domination, some 14,000 Afrikaners loaded their ox-drawn covered wagons and embarked on a 1,000-mile migration inland in 1837. This migration, known as the Great Trek, became a defining myth of Afrikaner history. The pioneers, or Voortrekkers, fought fierce battles with black Africans encountered along the way. The Great Trek further encouraged the Afrikaners' mystic belief in their own destiny—and their hostility toward blacks.

1846-1947
Independence

"Every sea in the world is being furrowed by ships conveying British troops from every corner of the globe in order to smash this little handful of people."—Jan Christiann Smuts, Afrikaner general (1899)

Southern Africa, blessed with gold, diamonds, and other mineral wealth, became a prized possession of the British. Overnight, the rough mining towns of Johannesburg and Cape Town sprang up on what was once empty grassland.

The British moved to add the inland mining regions to their empire, but the Afrikaners resisted. What became known as the Boer War erupted in 1899.

The Afrikaners won early victories but the more powerful British turned the tide. They interned 150,000 Afrikaner civilians in camps, where epidemics broke out and killed 26,000 prisoners. The Afrikaners were forced to surrender in 1902.

But the British, like the Afrikaners, considered only whites to be capable of self-government. When Britain gave the colony its independence in 1910, Afrikaners were allowed to dominate the government. Blacks were barred from voting and Afrikaans was made the official language.

There were also the first stirrings of opposition to Afrikaner rule. In 1912, a young Indian lawyer living in Cape Town named Mohandas K. Gandhi became outraged after being thrown off a train for sitting in a "whites only" seat. He organized a protest march, inspiring some black South Africans to form a civil rights organization. It was called the African National Congress (ANC).

Gandhi would later use his tactics of nonviolent civil disobedience to help bring about India's independence in 1948.

1948-1959
Rise of Apartheid

"Whatever the rights of the natives may be, they have no right to call on us to do anything that might jeopardize our supremacy."—J. B. M. Hertzog, founder of the National Party (1948)

From the time of the Europeans' arrival, South Africa had been a racist society. But in 1948, with the election victory of the Afrikaner-dominated National Party, racism became the official state ideology and governed every aspect of South African life. That ideology was called "apartheid"—Afrikaans for "apartness."

Many National Party members had been supporters of Germany's Nazi Party, a racist movement that had divided humanity into a German "master race" and other, "inferior" peoples to be enslaved.

Similarly, the South African Nationalists classified all citizens as either "white," "black," or "colored." Marriage or sexual relations across color lines became illegal. Separate residential areas were set up, with the whites getting the best land. Blacks saw their homes bulldozed and were forced into impoverished, crowded areas that were called "homelands," even though they had never lived there. These "homelands" covered 13 percent of South Africa's land area—for 75 percent of its population. "The goal," said Cornelius Mulder, a South African minister of black affairs, "is that eventually there will be no black South Africans."

Economic development was outlawed in the "homelands," and the only work remained in the white areas. Blacks were forced to endure long bus rides to work, or else live apart from their families in single-sex workers' barracks for most of the year. While they were in white areas, they were required to carry identification passes at all times. Despite these laws, 5 million blacks were desperate enough to live illegally in South Africa's white cities.

All public places in South Africa were segregated by race. Blacks were intentionally sent to inferior schools, since the only jobs open to them were as manual laborers.

1960-1975
Resistance to Apartheid

"I have fought against white domination, and I have fought against black domination. I have cherished the idea of a democratic and free society in which all persons live in harmony . . . It is an ideal which I hope to live for and to achieve. But if needs be, it is an ideal for which I am prepared to die."—Nelson Mandela, after being sentenced to life imprisonment (1964)

During the 1950s, apartheid's opponents of all races waged a lonely, dangerous, but nonviolent struggle. Then, in 1960, a black resistance group, the Pan Africanist Congress (PAC), called on blacks to defy the pass laws. Thousands of people in the black township of Sharpeville did so by marching to the police station and turning in their passes. Police opened fire, killing 69 and wounding 180 in what became known as the Sharpeville Massacre.

Until Sharpeville, anti-apartheid groups like the PAC and the ANC had supported nonviolent protests. Now, the government outlawed all of those groups. Arguing that they had no choice but to give up nonviolence, the ANC created an armed resistance movement, called "Spear of the Nation." Its leader was a young lawyer named Nelson Mandela.

In 1964, Mandela and the rest of the ANC's leaders were arrested and convicted of sabotage, and sentenced to life imprisonment. During his 26-year imprisonment, Mandela's work was carried on by his wife, Winnie, who herself was spied on, kidnapped, and repeatedly forced to move by police. Meanwhile, tens of thousands of apartheid opponents were arrested, detained, beaten, and in some cases, killed.

Although all black organizations were banned and their leaders in jail or exile, new ones soon sprang up. Unlike the ANC, which was open to all races and called for a multiracial South Africa, these new groups took their inspiration from Black Power groups in the U.S. They believed that blacks needed to unite and develop their own identity to confront whites as equals. Called the Black Consciousness Movement, its strongest appeal was to black youth. "We can never wage any struggle without offering a strong counterpoint to the white racism that permeates our society so effectively," declared Steven Biko, the movement's most charismatic and popular leader. In 1977, Biko was arrested and tortured. He died while in police custody. He was 30 years old.

1976-Present
The Fall of Apartheid
"Remember those who died when you vote and get elected. Think of those who died when you govern the country. When you celebrate and rejoice, when you march and sing, remember those who died."—Mzwakhe Mbuli, poet and musician (1992)

One law of apartheid held that all South African students be taught in Afrikaans. In 1976, students in Soweto, a black township in Johannesburg, poured into the streets to protest the rule. They regarded Afrikaans as the language of their oppressors.

The Soweto students had no recognized leaders, but their protest took hold and escalated into a demand for equal education with whites and an end to apartheid. The government responded by killing more than 600 students and arresting thousands. A new generation was imprisoned, sent into exile, and embittered.

In 1983, another wave of student-led protests rocked the nation, after a so-called electoral reform bill that excluded blacks passed the white parliament. Protests and strikes erupted across the country.

The government responded by declaring a state of emergency. Some 30,000 blacks were jailed, and the press was censored.

But this time, the system of apartheid had begun to crack. Unlike in the past, the government was not able to end the protests. And abroad, countries that had looked the other way during previous crackdowns voiced outrage.

Pressure Mounts

South Africa had been expelled from the United Nations in 1974, and from the Olympic Games in 1976. Then, in 1986, the U.S. Congress banned new investment by U.S. companies in South Africa. And around the world, governments moved to divest, or pull out, their investments from South Africa.

Facing immense pressure both at home and abroad, the Nationalists under President F. W. de Klerk slowly began repealing the apartheid laws. And in 1989, de Klerk secretly began negotiations with the jailed Nelson Mandela. On February 11, 1990, Mandela and his imprisoned colleagues were freed.

Over the next four years, de Klerk, the probable last white leader of South Africa, and Mandela, the probable first black leader, together negotiated an agreement to end apartheid and create a constitution for a new nonracial South Africa.

For their efforts, the two men won the 1993 Nobel Peace Prize. Accepting the award on December 10, 1993, Mandela declared: "We live with the hope that as she battles to remake herself, South Africa will be like a microcosm of the new world that is striving to be born."

Ettagale Blauer

Children of Apartheid

*A few months before South Africa's first free
elections, five South African teenagers were asked to
comment on the "new" South Africa and share their
experiences of the old apartheid system.*

***Agrineth Lekalakala, 17, Zulu. She is a senior in high school
and lives in the black township of Soweto, near Johannesburg.***
I'm very proud of what is going on in South Africa. I watch the news
every day with my parents and friends, and we talk about the election.
After we get the vote, I hope things will be better in Soweto. A lot of
people who lived in my neighborhood have moved away. They think
it's very dangerous—although I don't think so. What's true is people
don't think much of girls here. A lot of girls my age get pregnant and
drop out of school.

I'm part of the Bayeza Cultural Dancers—Bayeza means 'we are
going' in Zulu. I've been in the group three years. We are all under 18
years old. We do mixed African dances—Zulu and Xhosa. Being in
the group gets me off the streets. In December, we went to Orlando
Stadium in Soweto to dance for Heroes Day [a celebration that honors
those killed in the anti-apartheid struggle].

I'd like to go to college. I just finished my exams and I'm waiting
for the results. But we missed a lot of school this year [because of
demonstrations and boycotts], so I don't know how good the results
will be. And I'll need a scholarship to go.

I'm looking for work while I wait for my test results. I want to
work so I can help my family. We have no money. My mother was a
nurse, but she had an accident. My father was working but he lost his
job. They have to support me, one brother, and two sisters—and my
mother adopted two children who lost their parents.

Even if I don't get into university, nothing is impossible for me. I feel I can do whatever I feel like doing.

Annelise Faure, 18, colored. She is in her first year at the University of the Western Cape in Cape Town.
After the election, things are going to get worse. Blacks will treat whites the way they were treated. They don't say anything about the coloreds. We are in the middle. If it wasn't for [President] de Klerk, nothing would have changed. That's why I'm going to vote for the National Party. I think it's best for us. We are definitely afraid of the ANC [African National Congress]. They make a lot of promises to get votes. But they will do whatever they want to do.

Right now, they [the ANC] are arguing about the university. They want to lower standards and let a lot more people in. It's going to ruin the university. The Africans want it all now. They can't wait. They think only they suffered. But we suffered too. My brother was trained as a civil engineer but he couldn't get a job in his field. He had to take a job as a pipefitter. Before, all the jobs were for whites. Now they're going to be only for blacks. They don't think about us.

On New Year's I went to a midnight service at my church. It's the Dutch Reformed Church. The Church is very important to my family. We prayed, because we're very concerned about what will happen. Apartheid might be off the books but it's not off the mind. I think the AWB [extreme right-wing Afrikaners] will cause trouble. They won't accept blacks or whites who vote for de Klerk. Coloreds have no place else to go.

Marianneke Zondstra, 15, Afrikaner. She is a high school student in Somerset West, Cape Province.
I'm in my first year in high school. I speak Afrikaans, English, and Dutch. My parents are Dutch; they came here 30 years ago, but my brother and I were born in Cape Town.

My school used to be all white. Now, it's open to all races. The school is two-thirds white and one-third other races. Most of the others are colored. There are a few blacks. Now I have friends from all races. Three years ago, you were never around them; you didn't even know about them. Now you learn not to judge someone just by how they look.

Stories make South Africa sound a lot worse than it really is. The more people visit here the more they will find out what the country is really like. I think it's a great country. I have pen friends from all over the world and I try to tell them about what it's really like living here.

My parents have talked about going back to Holland. It was a real possibility at one point, but now they've decided to stay. I've been to Holland on a visit and they knew I really didn't want to go there. We talked about the Heidelberg Inn explosion [a terrorist bombing in December that killed three white people in Cape Town]. They're worried because it was a place that university students hang out in. They caution me about where I go. But you just have to carry on and hope you don't get caught up in the violence.

Carmen Fernandis, 14, colored. She is a junior high school student in Johannesburg.
We're able to go to better schools now that apartheid has been abolished. They have far better equipment, and far better teaching. The classes are smaller and teachers can spend time with each student. Everything is better, and it happened because for the first time we are able to choose the schools we want to attend.

Before, we didn't have a choice about what languages to take. I'm taking English and I'm still taking Afrikaans, but I think it will be abolished in a few years.

There are public schools standing empty [in Johannesburg] that were built for whites. They overbuilt in the minority areas. In the Cape, the black majority are taking over the schools that are standing empty. In some places, where there were no schools standing, the pupils have started teaching themselves.

I spend a lot of time playing sports. I'm in a softball tournament and my team has won two games against teams from two other provinces. A few years ago we wouldn't have been able to use this field because it was reserved for whites.

Tulani Xakekile, 16, Xhosa. He is a high school student in Langa Township, Cape Town.
I've been playing the xylophone since I was 6. I've been with this group, Heshoo Beshoo, for seven years. Heshoo Beshoo is slang—it means "going by force." Playing music is basically all I do, although I do plan to study some more.

Not much has changed since the end of apartheid. Change will come, but I don't see it yet. There have been a lot of promises. People have been promising that we will get more jobs. I'm not old enough to vote yet. I have six older brothers and sisters and they will vote, but they don't think it will be paradise. They think change in South Africa will go through many stages.

I was in the U.S. when my group toured there in 1991 and 1993. We were part of a children's festival. I was away for five weeks. I liked the way people live in the U.S. When you went into the shops, people did not look at your skin. I feel uncomfortable going into a shop in Cape Town. They look at me and think I'm going to take something.

We stay on our own and travel in our own combi [minivan] so we have less hassles. A lot of our music comes out of our own traditions, like a song about boys coming out of initiation school. Another song is, "There shall be no more tears." It's a song for all the people who have sacrificed themselves and left the country because of apartheid. It's dedicated to the new South Africa.

Judy Boppell Peace

from The Boy Child Is Dying

Over the many years that apartheid existed, people of both races came to have certain expectations of one another. In this story, a new kind of relationship develops between two women, one black and one white.

1

SHE STOPPED SPEAKING, looked at me and said, "Yes, I'll work for you."

Startled, I realized who had been interviewing whom. She had been introduced to me as Esther. "What is your last name?" I asked.

"Why do you want to know?" she responded.

"Simply because I am twenty-five years old, you are at least fifty and I would feel very uncomfortable having you call me Mrs. Peace while I called you Esther."

"I am Mrs. Esther Ntonsheni." She paused. "Mrs. Peace, I worked for a woman for ten years and she never knew I had any other name than Esther."

We had been in the apartment for a month. Having someone help me with my housework was not easy. I had always done my own work. I felt guilty watching someone else do it. Dick and I had decided that, for us, not having help was irresponsible. South Africa has something called "job reservation." Though this is breaking down slowly, for the majority of the black population it means finding a job is very difficult. And working as a house servant is still one of the easiest jobs to find. Since so many people need work, we reasoned, the least we could do was hire someone to help us.

We knew the "normal" working conditions. We had been told twelve rand (around seventeen dollars) a month was a good starting salary. Most people expected their servants to arrive around 7:30 A.M. and leave by 6:00 P.M., if they didn't live in. Servants considered themselves lucky to get an afternoon off a week. Many people felt they were being generous to give this, as it meant "managing on their own" that afternoon. We decided to ask Mrs. Ntonsheni to work a five-day week, from nine to five, with a salary above the norm. Perhaps this was one way of showing people around us new working possibilities.

Mrs. Ntonsheni entered the room. "Mrs. Peace, are you unhappy with my work?"

"No. Why do you ask?"

"Well, you are always doing it for me. I would prefer it if you left it to me!"

"I had not been sure how much to expect you to do, and I didn't want to overwork you," I replied, feeling slightly defensive.

"You are paying me a fair wage, giving me good hours and I want to feel I am earning my salary!"

Mrs. Ntonsheni took over the housework.

It wasn't more than three weeks later that Mrs. Ntonsheni said, "Mrs. Peace." I had come to recognize the tone. She had something to say. It was going to be difficult for her. She sounded defensive. "What have I done now?" I thought.

"Mrs. Peace, I have worked for white women many years—more than twenty. I was taught as a girl how to be in a white house. All the madams, they tell me I am a good servant. I do all I was taught for you. I think you don't like it. Why?"

I took a deep breath. I am not known for hiding my feelings and I too had been frustrated by our relationship. She was right. She had played the role of perfect servant, always "happy," constantly ready to please us. We could not have asked for more from a servant, and I assured her of this. "You do your job wonderfully well, Mrs. Ntonsheni. I couldn't ask for a better servant. Every morning, you are here punctually. 'I am fine,' you answer in response to my greeting. Your life is always fine. Yet I see traces of worry in your eyes. I see signs of suffering. I know your life cannot always be fine. You work hard, too hard. It is impossible to get you to rest. You feel guilty just sitting and relaxing for a few minutes.

When I enter the room, you seem tense and I feel it is kinder to keep out of your way. Mrs. Ntonsheni, I didn't hire you to be a servant under me. I hired another human being to help me with my work. I don't feel comfortable in the master/servant role. I'd like us to work at relating as two women—equals. I'm beginning to understand a little how hard that will be for you, but I'd like to try."

A few days later Mrs. Ntonsheni shouted from the kitchen, "Mrs. Peace, are you busy?"

"Not very. Why?"

"Well, I'm ironing and it is starting to rain and there are clothes on the line." A long pause.

"I'll get them," I said, as I left my letters and went out the back door, grabbing the clothes basket from the kitchen corner on the way.

"Whew, that rain is really coming down." I stamped my feet, shook my hair and plopped down the basket. Mrs. Ntonsheni gave me a long, searching look. It was no light thing she had done. I appreciated the risk she had taken and the beginning of trust it showed.

"Thank you," I said.

She nodded and I left the room.

2

South Africa is lovely beyond description: open veld, rolling hills, grand mountains, rugged coastline, flowers and foliage beautiful to behold. To explore and experience the sheer lushness and infinite variety of the land is pure pleasure. We spent delightful days trekking through game reserves, canoeing down quiet rivers, climbing mountain trails, searching out bushman paintings and hidden springs. The beaches of South Africa are some of the finest in the world, miles of white glistening sand bordering the warm waters of the Indian Ocean and the harsher waters of the Atlantic. Here are places to relax and be refreshed.

"Mrs. Ntonsheni, would you like to go to the beach with us this Saturday?"

Eyes sparkle. "I've never seen the ocean. Yes, I'd like to go."

"You have lived forty miles from the ocean most of your life and have never seen it?"

"Never had a way to get there." Her eyes slowly dulled. "I can't go with you," she said. "For a moment I forgot."

"Why not?"

"I'm not allowed on the white beaches. You would have to drive ten miles out to the 'non-European beach' and leave me there. I wouldn't enjoy being alone in a strange place. I would be allowed to stay with you on the white beach as a nanny to the children, but people would stare at me. I would feel uncomfortable. I wouldn't be allowed to put my feet in the water either. No, it is impossible for me to come with you."

Saturday came and we went to the sea. The relaxing warmth of sun on sand felt uncomfortably hot that day. The simple pleasure of play on the beach had become an escape from the harsh realities of a sick society, a place for the ostrich to stick his head in the sand.

3

We pulled into the drive-in restaurant. We stopped at one as often as possible when Mrs. Ntonsheni was in the car. We could not go into a restaurant together—one of the inconveniences of "petty apartheid." We ordered and settled back to wait, grateful for the chance to break our journey.

"Which order is for the girl?" the man at the car window asked Dick for the second time.

"Which girl do you mean? We have two daughters," said Dick. Jenny and Lisa romped together in the back seat oblivious to the conversation.

"You know what I mean." The man glared at us.

"No," Dick persisted politely, "I don't know what you mean."

The man took a deep breath. His face was flushed. His discomfort was evident. He pointed accusingly at Mrs. Ntonsheni.

"That girl!" There, he'd said it. He relaxed his breath and almost smiled.

"You couldn't possibly mean Mrs. Ntonsheni. She is at least fifty years old."

"You knew I meant her."

"No, I expected you to know the difference between a woman and a girl," said Dick. "My mistake."

"Which is her order," asked the man.

"What possible concern is that to you?" Dick replied.

"Natives cannot be served on our regular dishes. She has to have a tin plate and cup." The man was quick to catch the horror and disbelief that crossed our faces. "Nothing personal," he hastened to assure us. "We would lose customers if we didn't enforce this policy."

The man stood alone in the car space as the five customers he had just lost drove away.

My anger sputtered over in irrational statements and oaths against apartheid.

"Mrs. Peace, don't let yourself get so upset. You aren't hurting that man or the system or anyone but yourself. That was a minor incident for me. One of many I encounter in the course of a day. If I allowed myself to feel anger every time I was treated that way, I would be a sick woman by now."

"It was so stupid, so wrong, so humiliating," I said.

"Yes, it was."

"How can you sit back and do nothing? Don't you care if you have to live this way?"

"It is my daily prayer to see this country change. Anything that brings a good change, I am for. But useless anger, destructive violence—that hurts me more than the man who calls me girl."

Years later Dick talked with a man in Cape Town. He was a "Cape colored" who had been thrown out of his home. There was a lovely section of the Cape which had been a colored area for three generations. A community of neatly kept, colorful cottages along the coast of the Indian Ocean. The government decided it would make a nice resort for the white community. The area was reclassified as a white area. The colored people, many had lived there all their lives, were moved *en masse* to a new location: a dry, sandy spot where forty m.p.h. winds whip the sand mercilessly into eyes, nose and throat, making the soulless concrete rooms called homes seem almost havens. The new colored area is miles from Cape Town. People ride buses for an hour to get to work.

"How do you stand this?" Dick asked his friend.

"The first year, I nearly went insane. I woke from the little sleep I'd get to a sense of fury, frustration, hatred. There came a morning when I didn't want to wake up. My bitterness had eaten away my desire for life. The injustice that had been dealt me and my people was beyond my capacity to endure. 'This,' I said to myself, 'is not smart. The white men are enjoying our homes. My hatred is not touching them. It only poisons me. Once I loved life, now I despise it.' I decided then that I would look at life again and accept the gifts of each day. I work all I can for the coming of a just society for my land, but I cannot afford the luxury of hating my oppressors. I think I have come to pity them instead."

4

South Africa exists to a large degree by grace of the mine workers. Without the revenue from the gold mines, the economy would grind to a halt. Every year thousands of black men leave their homes to work in the mines. The homelands are places of children, women and old men. The young men give their youth and vitality away in the dark underground caverns which yield the precious metal. When we were in South Africa, they received in return for the strength of their manhood approximately a dollar a day.

For eleven months of the year, men are herded together into dormitories "according to their tribes." The government claims they are "preserving cultural identities" in this way. It is a small coincidence that it also keeps the blacks of South Africa from feeling a strong national identity. History does continue to move forward, and that national identity is growing in spite of the government's concern for "nourishing one's tribal roots."

All manner of social problems arise from the housing situation. Picture hundreds of men sharing bunks in crowded barracks; some bunks made of concrete with no mattresses. No family life, no male-female relationships, no nurture from the earth each lived with most of his childhood. Much crime and prostitution take place, giving rise to the myth of the immoral, irresponsible black man.

"How can our natives stand to live like that? If anyone doubts the black man is different from the white, he only has to see what goes on in those mine compounds. A white man couldn't survive there!"

Jim, a friend, arrived at a suburban Johannesburg home. The hostess had provided an elegant, bountiful table for her guests. The host, a mine executive, was in an expansive mood. The evening was warm, the guests mellow, content. The host raised his glass of superb South African wine.

"A toast to South Africa, our beloved land. Where else in the world could we enjoy life as fully and live so well?"

The people smiled, nodded, clinked their glasses and looked out over the manicured, well-lighted garden.

"I would be interested in the opinions of your mine workers lying on their cold, hard bunks, as to the benefits of being a South African tonight," said Jim.

The easy silence had been broken, the evening tarnished. Jim was not invited back.

5

Too soon our years in South Africa were coming to an end. This had been our place for eight years—our first home together after our marriage, the land of our daughter's birth. We knew it was time to leave, yet we knew we would be leaving much of ourselves behind.

Mrs. Ntonsheni and I avoided the subject, until one day she looked at me. "What can I say to you? You are taking my babies away from me."

"I know," I said. "You are as much a part of their lives as we are. You have given so much of yourself to them and have enriched their lives beyond measure. What can I say to you to ease the pain of their leaving? There is nothing that will make it easy. I don't know how I can leave you myself. We have known one another and worked together for eight years. I don't let myself think of our going."

"Mrs. Peace, we must both think of your going. The time is coming. I will have to work for someone when you leave. My children must eat and go to school. We must think about where I will work. It is better for me to find a new job before you go."

"I have thought of that. I think I can find you a job with one of our friends before we go."

Mrs. Ntonsheni shook her head. "You will not find me a job with your friends."

"Why not? They all know how responsible you are."

"They also see how I am in your house. They will not want me to behave the same in their houses."

"Mrs. Ntonsheni, you are too cynical. Our friends cannot help but see what a good worker you are. They may have changed their perspectives by observing us together."

"I am not cynical, just realistic. You can try to find me a job with one of your friends, but you will fail. Many of them are nice people, but most of them are white South Africans first."

I spent the next few weeks informing friends that Mrs. Ntonsheni needed a job starting the first of July. Some said they would have her if they needed help, which they didn't. A few said they needed help, but wouldn't have her. They preferred having someone they felt comfortable training in the ways of their household. They felt Mrs. Ntonsheni had "too strong a personality" to fit into a different lifestyle. I tried, but

I was unable to find Mrs. Ntonsheni a job. I finally accepted defeat and placed an ad in the local paper. "Responsible black woman wants housework. Excellent references available." With excellent references, it is not hard to find work. Mrs. Ntonsheni soon had the security of a monthly paycheck once we were gone.

The day we were to leave arrived. How does one leave a place that has been home and people who have been friends. The time had come for Mrs. Ntonsheni and me to say goodbye.

I looked at Mrs. Ntonsheni.

"Life is made up of meeting and parting, of saying hello and good-bye," she said, and looked away.

"How can I leave you?" I thought to myself. We had been together for eight years. We had felt anger and affection, cautiousness and trust, distance and warmth, frustration and enjoyment, depression and hope. We had felt alien to one another and we had felt known by one another. Our lives had become interdependent in so many ways, even while we had feared this. In eight years, we had come to love one another. I embraced Mrs. Ntonsheni. "I cannot say goodbye to you. It is too hard for me."

"It is too hard for me." she said. "I have dreaded the coming of this day."

We both wept.

She left me standing alone in the garden. Walking slowly, with head erect, she passed through the gate. She did not look back.

Ranjit Warrier

Jargon from ISL (ISLESE)

Spoken language in South Africa is sometimes a mixture of English, various Zambian languages, and Afrikaans. The following is a glossary of slang terms compiled by a student at the International School of Lusaka in Zambia.

ISL has a special language of its own. This language is a hybrid of English, various Zambian languages, and the occasional Afrikaans (from South Africa). This is a collection of some of the most popular ISLESE.

Bail out
To go to sleep.
Contributed by Rohit Sagar.

Bali
The origins are in the Indian language Gujarati. . . . everyone uses it in ISL when they're talking about their father. e.g. *My bali's getting a new car.*

Book out
To leave somewhere. e.g. *Eemwe, I'm booking out.*
Thanks to Rohit Sagar.

Boot
Boot is used when you play football, usually the most common word thrown at the goalkeeper by the members of the same team. It just means kick the ball as hard as you can so it goes the farthest possible distance.

Buta
Buta means brother and it is used mostly to call people whose names you don't know. Used as a replacement for a name and it makes the

person who you're talking to feel more comfortable with you because you've just called him a brother.

Crop
To crop means to fall down. This has been in use in Lusaka for a long time and is still going strong, especially among the UNZA people. You don't tend to hear it in ISL all that much these days. e.g. *I cropped bad kind yesterday on the football ground.* . . . I fell badly on the football ground yesterday.

Ekse, pronounced eksay
The most common slang in use at ISL. It comes from Afrikaans and originally meant, "I say." At ISL, it can be used to mean anything from "You're the greatest friend on Earth" to "I hate you and I wish you were dead." Most of the time, though, it is used as a word that bridges a gap in a sentence, when the speaker is thinking about what to say next. The trick to understanding when it means what is to listen to the tone in which it is said and its position in the sentence. e.g. *Ekse, I have to go ekse, to a class ekse, so ekse, see you ekse* . . . The first ekse refers to the other person, the next two are just words that filled pauses when the speaker would be thinking what to say, and the last two are referring to the other person. This is a simple example, usually ekse speech can get really complicated.

Fastele
Fastele is a cartoon character that appears in one of the local newspapers, *The Weekly Post*. ISL uses fastele to mean "fast." You would use it in any place where you would use fast or quick, and you don't have to change fastele to suit the tense. e.g. *I'm going to do this job fastele* . . . I'm going to do this job quickly.

Flat
Being flat is to be annoyed or upset or angry . . . one of those words that depends on how you say it to get the meaning. e.g. *Ekse, the 'un was flat when someone smashed his* G . . . I say, the guy was angry when someone smashed his car.
Courtesy of Nic Kotschoubey.

G
A G is a vehicle . . . usually a car. e.g. *I have the G ekse* . . . let's go. Thanks to Archit Mohindra for reminding me.

Glide
Glide means to ride somewhere in something . . . or simply to go. e.g.
Let's glide to Popeye's. . . . Let's drive to Popeye's.
Thanks to Archit Mohindra for reminding me.

Graze
To eat! e.g. *Ekse I missed the match coz I was grazing, I'll watch lusha's goal on sports results tonight* . . . I say, I missed the football game because I was eating. I'll watch Kalusha's goal on sports results tonight.
Courtesy of Nic Kotschoubey.

Hidjoooo
Hidjoooo! comes from one of the Zambian languages and means "here is," but is used as a form of emphasis. e.g. *When somebody does a nice shot in football, you can shout "hidjoooo!"*
Courtesy of Nic Kotschoubey.

Jol
Jol - to go somewhere
Thanks to Rohit Sagar.

Is iti tirue?/It isi tirue . . .
This is a question and the classic answer. It came from a famous song by a guy called Kachaka. The first day this song came on ZNBC, everyone all over Zambia who watched the song was asking everyone else, "Is iti tirue?" The proper response to this is, "It isi tirue." I still need some of the lyrics. "It isi tirue" is such a famous song because it is sung in a very exaggerated Zambian accent and is hilarious to say the least.

Ka, kama, chima, chimaka
At ISL we use ka, kama, chima, chimaka after the words the, that or this in a sentence. What you would do is attach one of these words to the noun . . . which word you attach depends on how much emphasis you want to put on the noun and how much respect you want to give the noun. Chimaka and ka have the most emphasis and the same amount of respect. This is very little respect, but more than what kama gives. Kama is the article which gives the noun the least respect and about medium emphasis. e.g. *The ka-table is in my way.* . . . *That kama-chalk won't write.* . . . *This chimaka pen doesn't have any ink.* The most emphasis here is on the pen, the least respect here

is assigned to the chalk. It gets easier when you actually hear it being used.

Kacheppa, pronounced slowly, syllable by syllable, with emphasis on the ka

This has a derogatory meaning in a local Zambian language, but at ISL, people use it to mean that someone circulates a lot of rumours. The origin of this word was in an advertisement on the beloved national channel, ZNBC, which showed KACHEPPA in big block letters (vendeckya aksharangal, for the malayalees out there) and talked about people who spread rumours. Of course this caught on and all the local rumour mongers were labelled as Kacheppa. It is used exactly like a name. e.g. *She's a real Kacheppa. . . . Kacheppa, what is this you have been saying?* As you can see, Kacheppa is just used to label someone's rumour-spreading trait.

Kuleebe, pronounced kuleebay

When I left, this word was catching on. It comes from one of the Zambian languages and it means, "nothing." ISL has adopted this word to mean "I don't have it" or "I don't know." Depending on how it is used in a sentence, it can also mean, "it isn't here."

Lekker, pronounced la- as in latter and -ka as in karate

This is a Dutch word from South Africa. It is used to mean "excellent" and can describe anything or anyone. e.g. *That's a lekker car, ekse. . . . it was a lekker movie.* These sentences mean "That's an excellent car," and "It was an excellent movie."

Mali/Queen

Mali is, of course, from Gujarati, and it means mom. . . . everyone uses it to mean mom. Queen is also used, but it is more commonly found in the Lake Road School language than in ISLese.

Mat

To put a car into maximum acceleration.
Thanks to Rohit Sagar.

Mwana

Mwana means friend . . . origins are in one of the local languages . . . used by "Lusakans" as other English speakers would use "man" or "my friend." e.g. *Mwana, did you see that merc?* . . . Man, did you see that Mercedes?
Courtesy of Nic Kotschoubey.

Nickis

Nickis comes from the German "nichts" and means "nothing," or "no," or any general word of negation. e.g. *"Is there any sugar left?"* *"Aaaah, nickis." "Did you find a taxi?" "Aaaah, nickis." "Go and do this for me ekse!" "NICKIIIIS!"*
Courtesy of Nic Kotschoubey.

Perch

To perch means to sit somewhere. e.g. *Perch here ekse* . . . I say, sit here.
Courtesy of Nic Kotschoubey.

Plastic

Plastic - doing something the wrong way.
Contributed by Rohit Sagar.

Prang

To prang means to crash something, usually a car. I started hearing it spoken in ISL from about '93 or so. e.g. *Don't prang the car.* . . . Don't crash the car.

Saat

A direct translation would be "No" but it is used as a more empathetic no. e.g. *Did you get the G? Saat, ekse, my brother tuned no.*
Thanks to Rohit Sagar for reminding me.

Yu-ay

A very rude way of calling someone. It comes from one of the Zambian languages and is in widespread use all over the country. Use it as you would, "hey, you!!"

Armando Valladares (är-män´dô bä-yä-dä´rĕs)

Translated by Marguerite Guzman Bouvard

They Have Not Been Able

People living under apartheid often felt like prisoners—many of the things they valued were taken from them. This poem, written by an imprisoned Cuban protester, expresses joy in those things that cannot be taken away.

They have not been able to take away
the rain's song
not yet
not even in this cell
5   but perhaps they'll do it tomorrow
that's why I want to enjoy it now,
to listen to the drops
drumming against
the boarded windows.
10 And suddenly it comes
through I don't know what crack
through I don't know what opening
that pungent odor
of wet earth
15 and I inhale deeply
filling myself to the brim
because perhaps they will also
prohibit that tomorrow.

No Han Podido

No han podido quitarme
todavía
en este encierro
el canto de la lluvia
5   pero quizás lo hagan mañana
por eso quiero ahora disfrutarlo
escuchar las gotas
más allá de mis ojos
y los esperos muros
10   golpear con insistencia
las ventanas tapiadas.
Y de pronto me llega
no sé por qué ranura
no sé por qué intersticio
15   ese olor agradable
de la tierra mojada
y la aspiro muy hondo
para llenarme bien
porque quizás también
20   lo prohiban mañana.